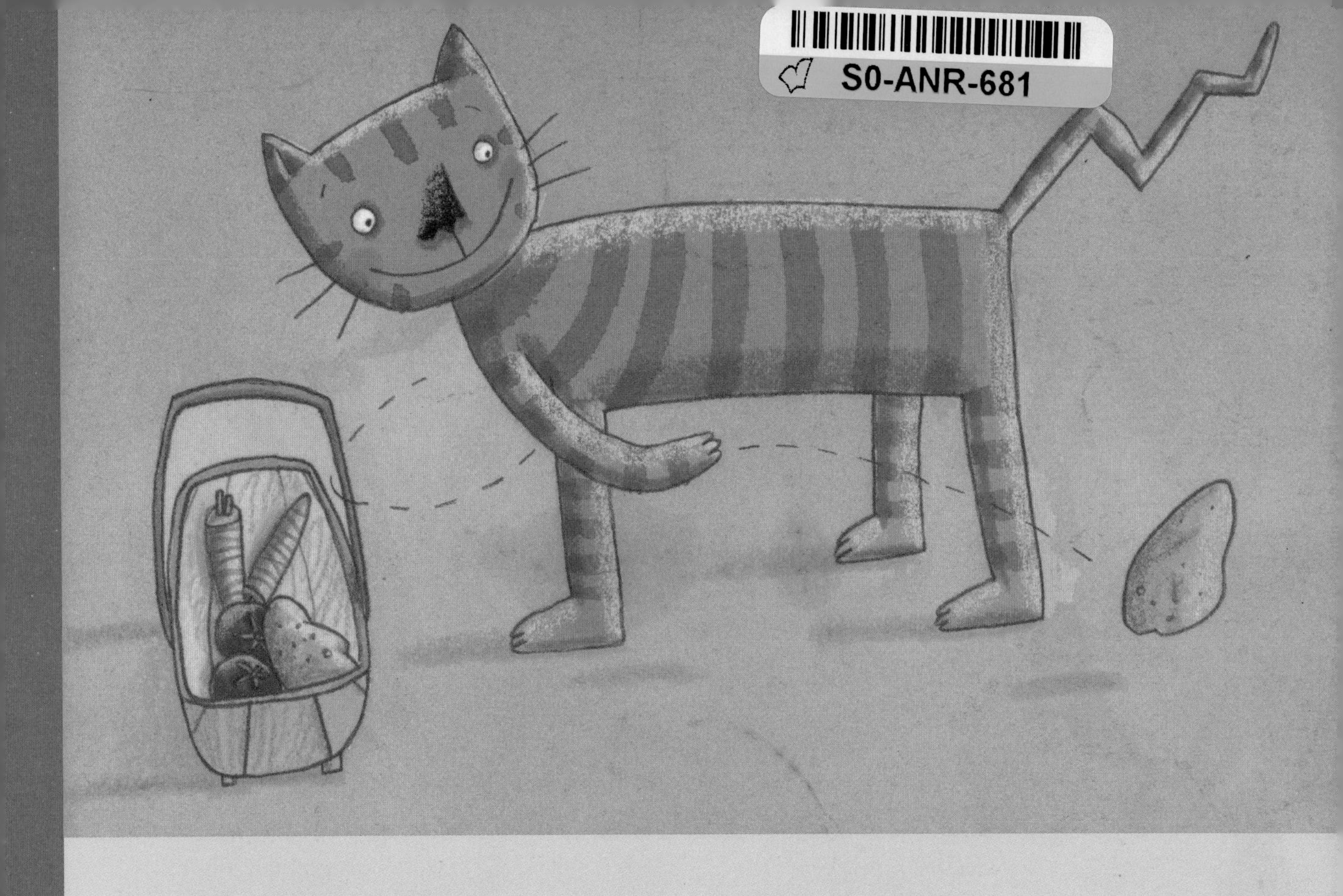

Tabby Cat swats a potato.

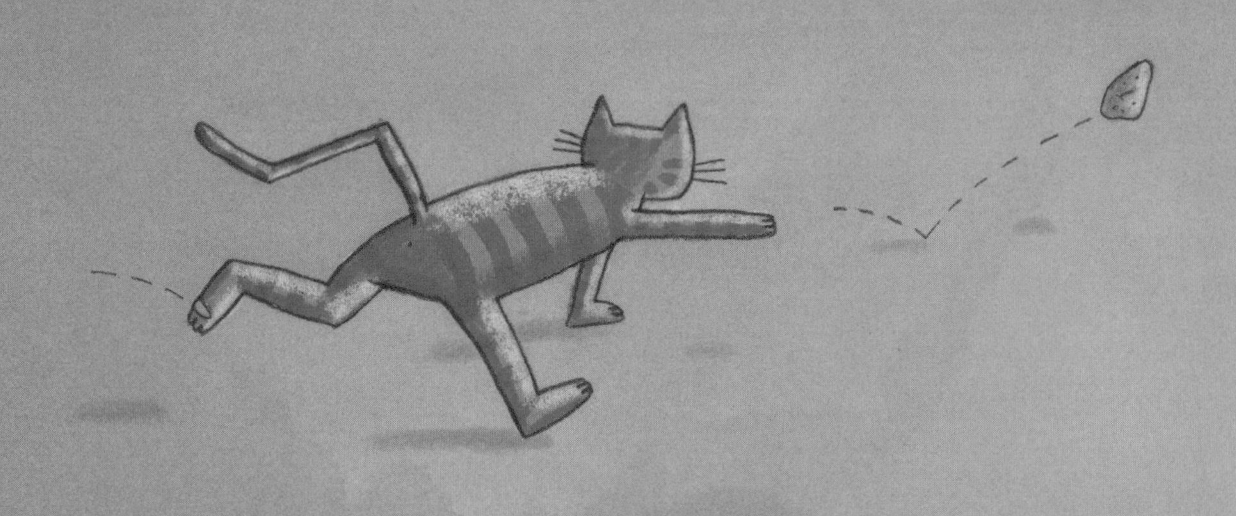

BUMP! Away goes the potato.

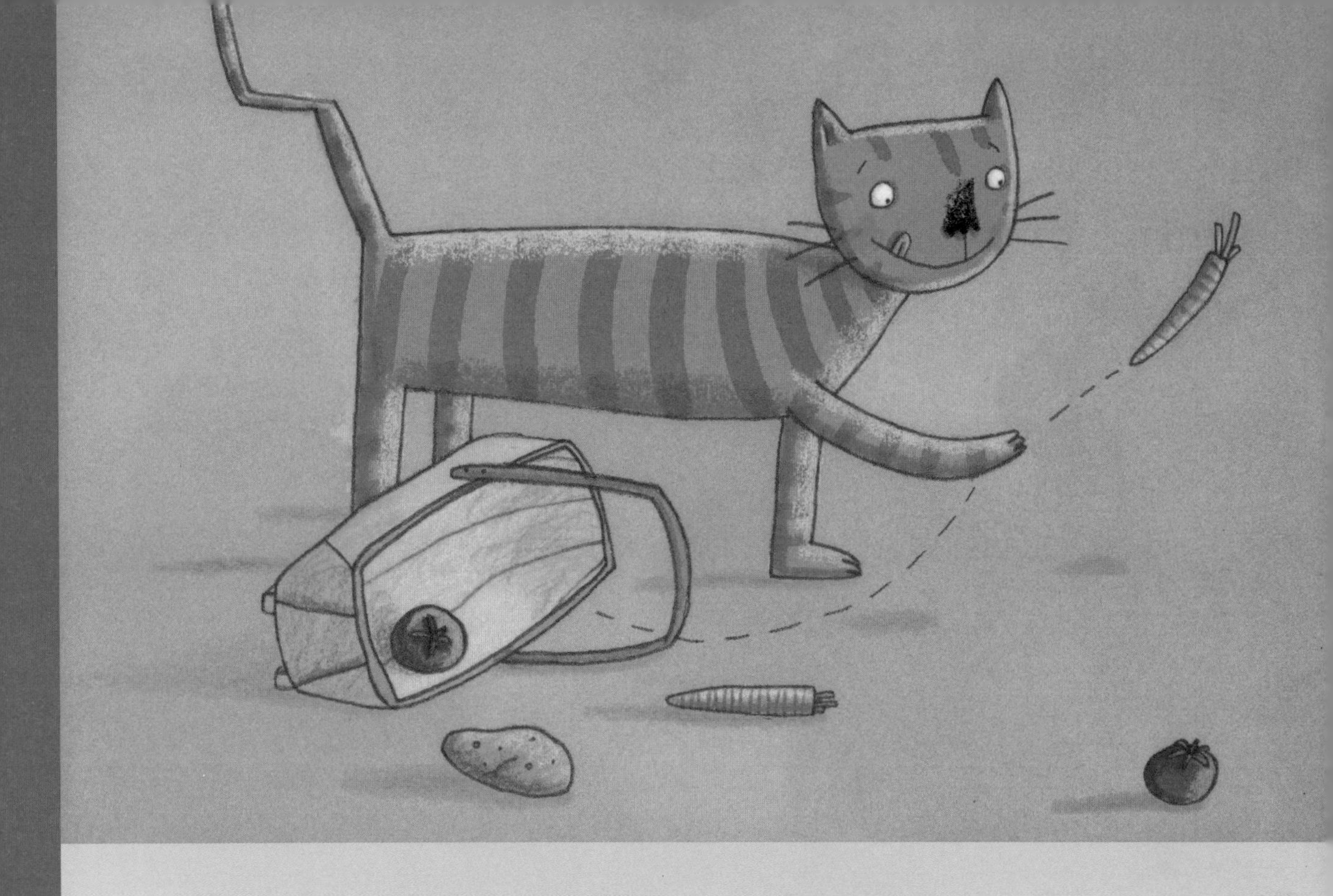

Tabby Cat swats a carrot.

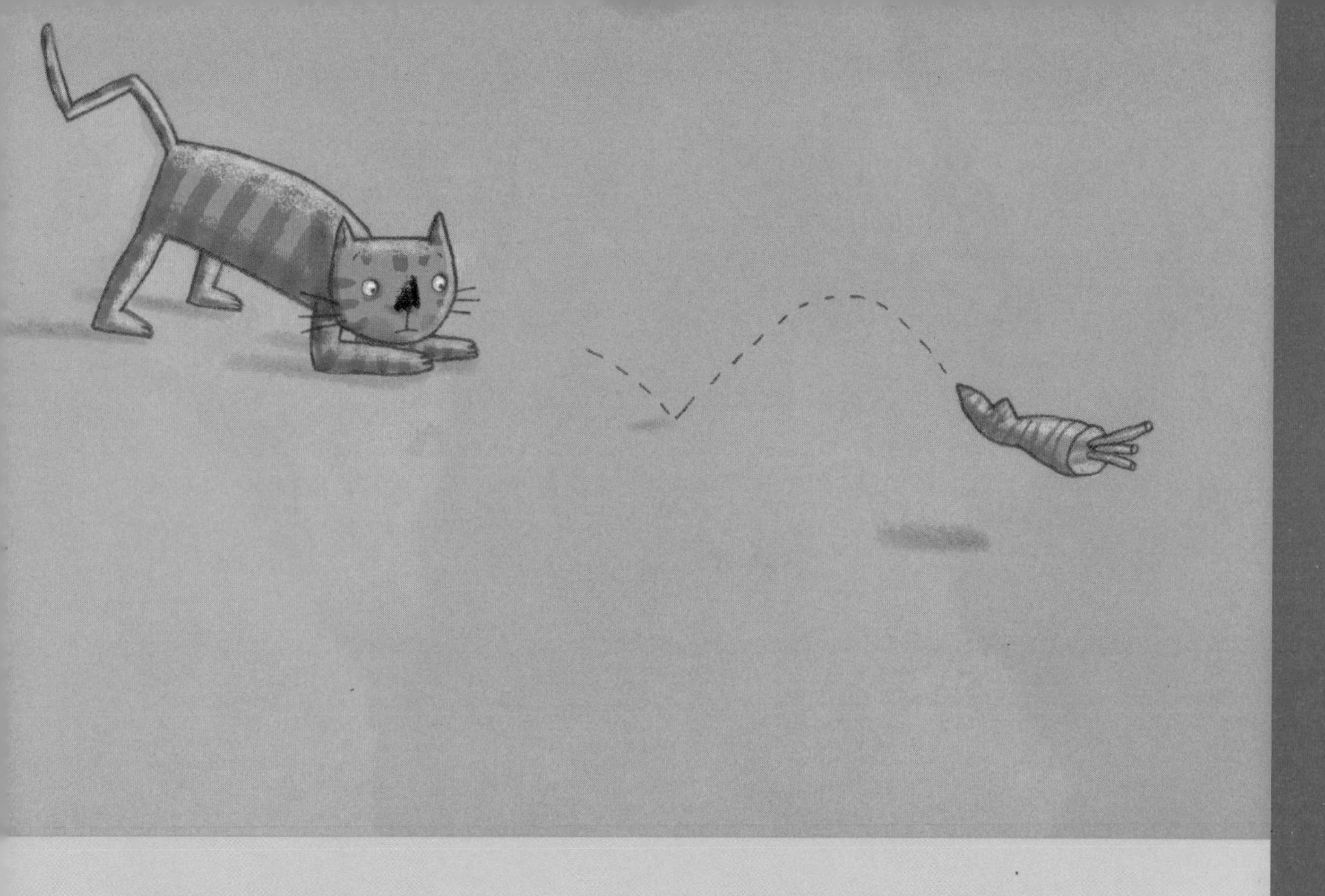

THUMP! Away goes the carrot.

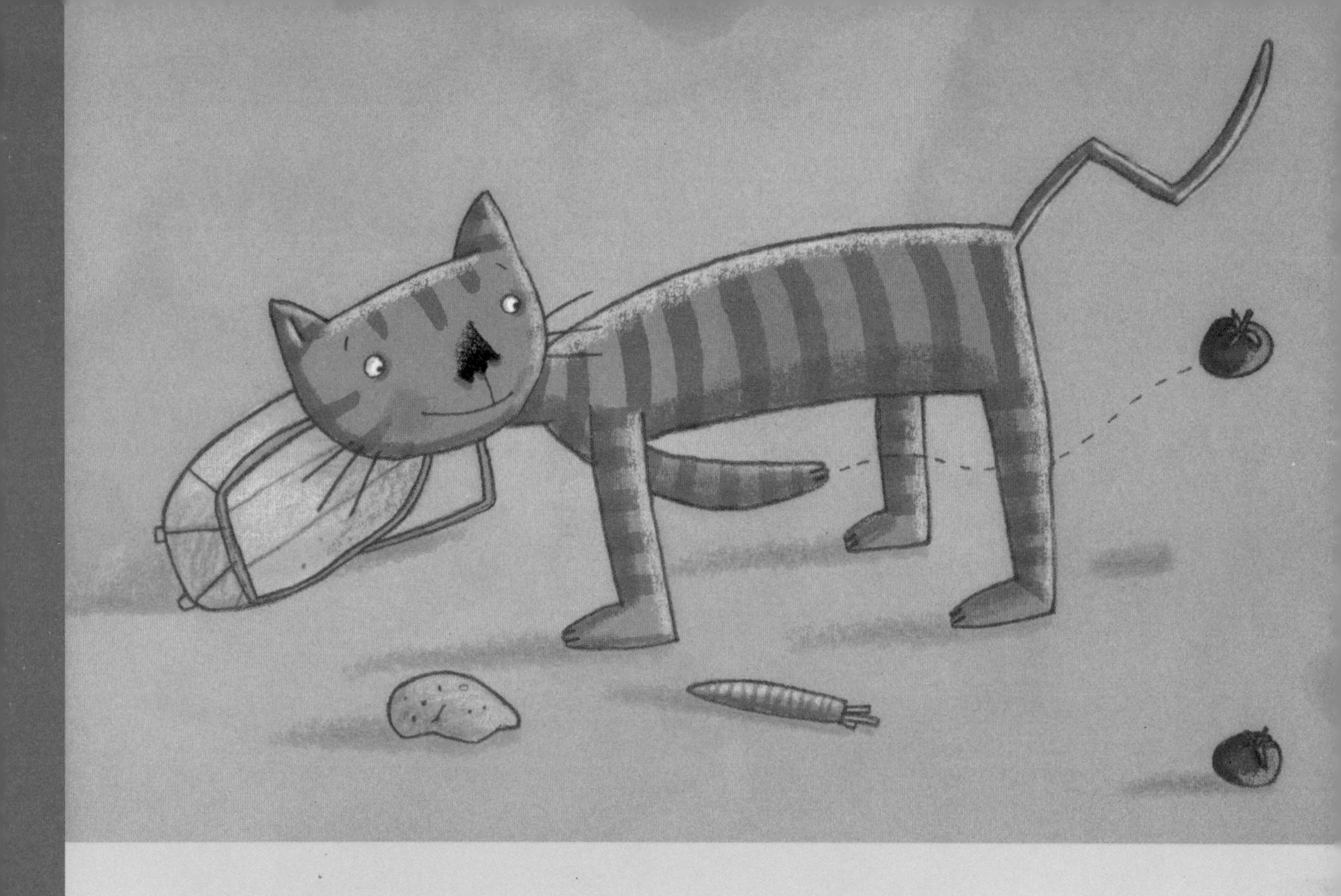

Tabby Cat swats a tomato.

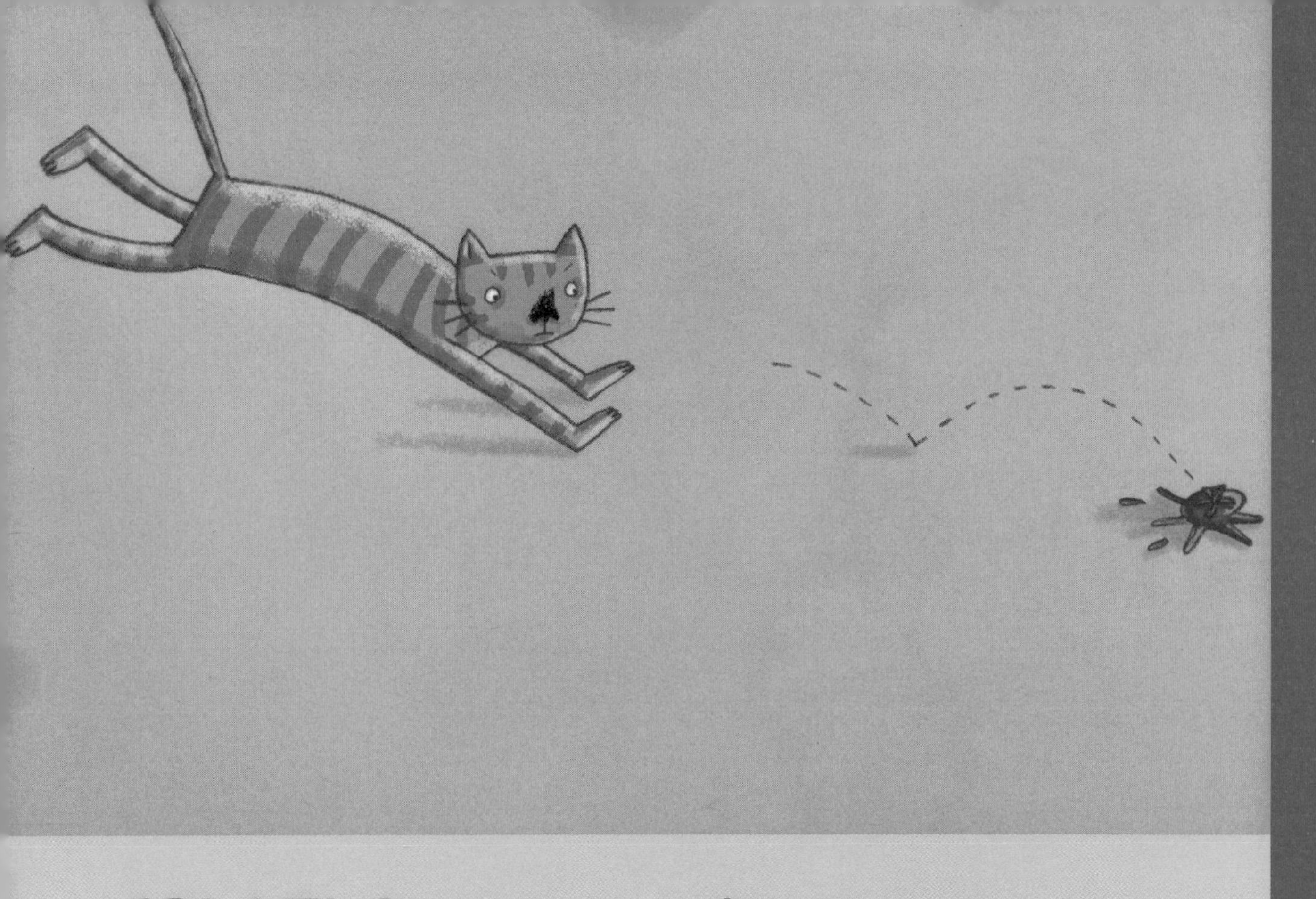

SPLAT! Away goes the tomato.

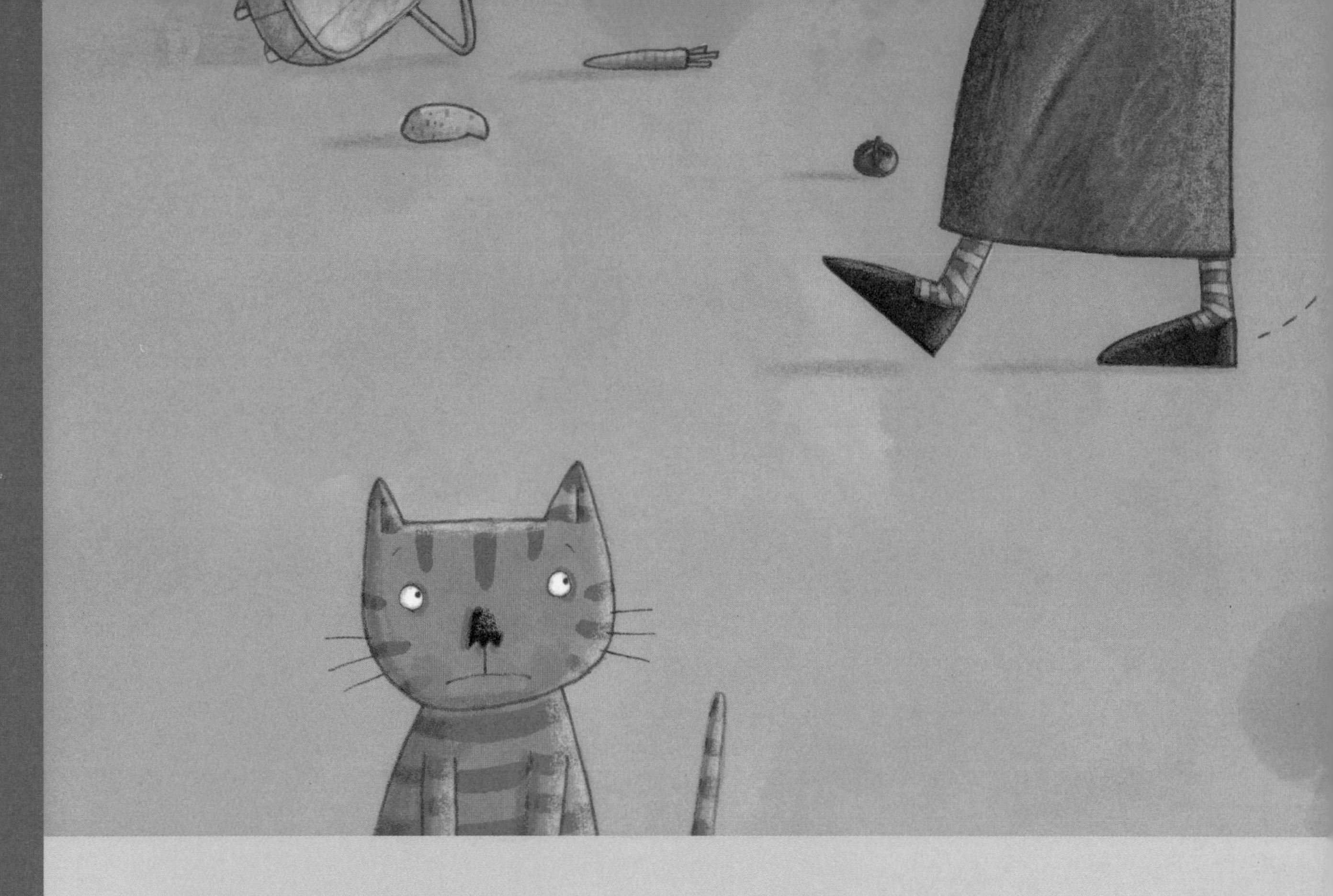

Oh, oh! Here comes Mommy!

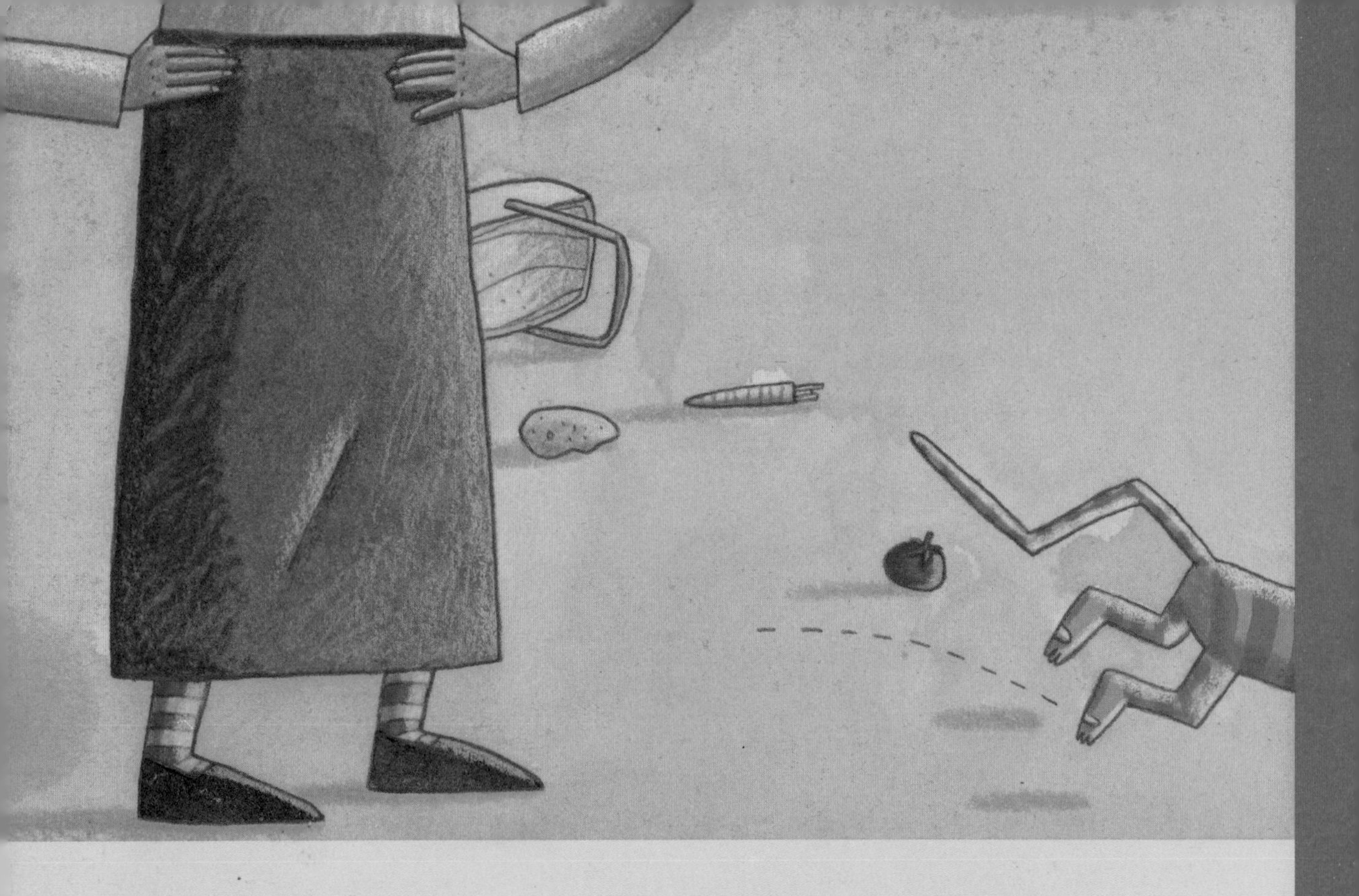

SCAT! Away goes Tabby Cat.